You can be a Brownie Girl Scout, too!

If you are 6, 7, or 8 years old, or in the 1st, 2nd, or 3rd grade, just ask your parents to look in your local telephone directory under "Girl Scouts," and call for information. You can also ask your parents to call **Girl Scouts of the U.S.A.** at **1-(212) 852-8000** or write to 420 Fifth Avenue, New York, NY 10018-2702 to find out about becoming a Girl Scout in your area.

For the Brownie Girl Scouts
of Maplewood, New Jersey,
and with thanks to Cornelia — M.L.

To my Johansen ancestors,
who were lighthouse keepers
and sailing ship captains — L.S.L.

Copyright © 1995 by Girl Scouts of the United States of America. All rights reserved. Published by Grosset & Dunlap, Inc., a member of The Putnam & Grosset Group, New York, in cooperation with Girl Scouts of the United States of America. GROSSET & DUNLAP is a trademark of Grosset & Dunlap, Inc. Published simultaneously in Canada. Printed in the U.S.A.

Library of Congress Cataloging-in-Publication Data

Leonard, Marcia.
    Lights out, Sarah! / by Marcia Leonard ; illustrated by Laurie Struck Long.
        p.   cm. — (Here come the Brownies ; 9)
    Summary: Sarah faces her fear of the dark when she goes on an overnight to an island lighthouse with her Brownie Girl Scout troop.
    [1. Fear of the dark—Fiction. 2. Lighthouses—Fiction. 3. Girl Scouts—Fiction.] I. Long, Laurie Struck, ill. II. Title.
III. Series.
PZ7.L549Lf   1995
[Fic]—dc20   94-39912

ISBN 0-448-40841-4   A   B   C   D   E   F   G   H   I   J

HERE COME THE BROWNIES
A Brownie Girl Scout Book

Lights Out, Sarah!

By Marcia Leonard
Illustrated by Laurie Struck Long

Grosset & Dunlap • New York
In association with GIRL SCOUTS OF THE U.S.A.

1

Sarah leaned against the deck rail of the Point Lucy ferryboat. A gentle breeze blew back her long, brown hair. She took a deep breath. The sea air smelled wonderful.

Sarah and the other Brownie Girl Scouts in her troop had spent the morning on a bus. They had left home very early, along with their leader, Mrs. Quinones, and several moms. Now everyone was crowded around Sarah, looking out to sea.

"This is so great!" said Jo Ann.

"Just wait. It's going to get even better," said Amy. "Tonight we'll be on our own private island!"

"And sleep in our own private lighthouse!" added Corrie.

"It's not *really* private," Krissy A. said, with a serious look. "The island's a state park. And the government runs the lighthouse."

Sarah smiled. Krissy A. always liked to get the facts straight.

"Well, we *are* the only visitors who get to sleep over," said Amy. "So after the last ferry leaves, we'll have the whole place to ourselves. Except for the park ranger."

"I wonder what it will be like," said Jo Ann. "I mean, sleeping on an island, so far away from everything."

"It'll be cool!" said Amy.

"It'll be dark too!" said Krissy A. "No city lights. It'll be just right for stargazing— if the sky is clear."

The girls talked about finding the Big Dipper and the North Star. But Sarah didn't join in. She was thinking about the dark.

Sarah was afraid of the dark. But she was too shy and embarrassed to tell her friends. Kids in second grade weren't supposed to be afraid of the dark anymore.

To make herself feel better, Sarah patted the pocket of her duffel bag. Yes, her little flashlight was still there. She took it with her on every Brownie overnight—just in case.

Tonight, Sarah would tuck the flashlight under her pillow. Then if she started to see strange things in the dark, she could switch it on—fast!

The ferry rounded a bend, and Sarah spied a large rocky island.

"Land, ho!" cried Amy. "There's our island. And there's the Point Lucy Lighthouse!"

Sarah could see it too! She shaded her eyes to see better.

The lighthouse was a tall, round, white tower. It had a glassed-in top with a balcony around it. And it stood on a rocky point of land, not far from the crashing waves.

"Look how tall the tower is," said Amy. "I'm going to climb to the very top!"

"Me too," said Sarah. "I bet you can see for a million miles from up there!"

Not far from the lighthouse was a group of smaller buildings. Some were new. But one was an old-fashioned cottage, with a bright red roof and lacy white trim.

"Look!" Krissy A. pointed to the house. "I wonder if that's where the lighthouse keeper lives."

"It's so cute!" said Corrie. "It looks like a dollhouse from here."

Mrs. Q. began rounding up the troop. "Grab your stuff," she called. "We're almost there."

Sarah grabbed her bag. She couldn't wait to go ashore and see everything!

The ferry slowed down as it got closer to the island. Then it gently bumped the dock. A moment later, the Brownies and the other visitors streamed off the deck.

A short, trim woman in a tan uniform was waiting to greet them. She had wind-blown gray hair and bright blue eyes.

"Welcome," she said, shaking hands with Mrs. Q. "Susan Blair, Park Ranger. Glad

you're here. Perfect day."
She squinted at the sky.
"May storm tonight.
Don't know yet.
Have to wait and see."

Sarah smiled.
Ranger Blair's sentences were
as short and trim as she was!

Some of the other girls had noticed
the same thing. They were smiling, too.

The ranger grinned back at them. "I
know," she said. "I never use ten words
when five will do. Guess I don't like to
waste them."

She picked up a big box of cooking
supplies that Mrs. Q. had brought along.
"Follow me," she called over her shoulder.

Sarah fell in line with the other girls.

Soon they passed the new buildings they

had seen from the ferry. Ranger Blair pointed to each one. "Ranger's quarters. Supply shed. Rest rooms—that one's important. No bathrooms in the lighthouse."

"We'll remember," said Mrs. Q.

The girls came to the little cottage. "Is this the lighthouse keeper's house?" Krissy A. asked.

"Was," said Ranger Blair. "It's a museum now. I'll give you the tour. But first, come meet the old girl." She led them around the side of the cottage.

The Brownies followed, looking puzzled. Who was the ranger talking about?

"There she is!" Ranger Blair said with pride. "Over one hundred and fifty years old. Still strong. Still beautiful. The Point Lucy Lighthouse."

2

The Point Lucy Lighthouse gleamed snowy white against the bright blue sky.

" 'Lucy' comes from the Latin word for 'light.' That's how she got her name," said Ranger Blair. She gave the painted stone wall a friendly pat. "Lucy's walls are seven feet thick here at the base, and she's over sixty feet high."

Sarah craned her neck to see the top. Up close, the tower seemed even taller than it had from the ferry.

"Yes, she's a fine old girl," Ranger Blair went on. "She's survived gales, hurricanes, snow, sleet, floods—you name it. And she's outlasted a dozen keepers."

"Are you the keeper now?" asked Corrie.

The ranger shook her head. "In the old days, Lucy had an oil lamp. And she needed a keeper to keep the flame going. But now her beacon runs on electricity, and it has a light sensor. That means when the sun goes down, the beacon comes on by itself. So Lucy doesn't need a keeper anymore."

Sarah noticed something. When Ranger Blair talked about the lighthouse, her sentences got longer. And she treated Lucy almost as if she were a person. Not just a building.

Sarah could see why Ranger Blair felt that way. The lighthouse seemed friendly

somehow. As the Brownies went inside,
Sarah gave the wall a pat, too.

"You'll be sleeping on the lowest floors,"
the ranger explained. She led the way up one
flight of stairs and through a door.

"Neat! A round room," said Krissy S. "I feel like a princess in a tower."

"Rapunzel, Rapunzel," Amy called out. Then she looked around the room. "Hey! How can you let down your hair? There's no window!"

"The windows are higher up," said the ranger. "Settle in. Then climb to the top, four girls at a time. I'll meet you up there."

Sarah and Jo Ann found a spot for their stuff. They were buddies for this trip. And buddies stuck together.

Sarah was glad to see Mrs. Q. put her things nearby. I am *not* going to be scared of the dark, she told herself. But it was nice to know that Mrs. Q. would be close.

When it was their turn, Sarah and Jo Ann climbed the stairs to the top of the tower. Amy and Krissy S. were right behind them.

Up and up they went.
Around and around. Sarah
was starting to get dizzy
when she finally reached
the glassed-in room.

The gray-blue sea
spread out before her.
A flock of gulls soared
over the water. And
there were four ships
like polka dots
on the horizon.

"Oh! How pretty!"
Sarah breathed.

"Yes, it is,"
said Ranger Blair.
"But deadly, too.
There are lots of big rocks

just below the surface. That's why Lucy's here. To warn sailors to stay clear as they come into the bay. Even so, storms sometimes drive boats onto the rocks."

"You mean they get wrecked?" Jo Ann asked.

The ranger nodded. "Many good ships have been lost off this coast. And many good sailors have drowned."

"That sounds like the beginning of a story," said Krissy S.

"Yeah, a *ghost* story!" said Amy.

"Well, some say that when there's a big storm, you can hear the cries of the sailors who've drowned," said Ranger Blair.

The girls' eyes grew wide.

"Me, I don't believe in ghosts. I think it's just the wind," the ranger went on.

"Anyway, I'd rather think about all the lives Lucy has *saved*."

"How many is that?" asked Jo Ann.

"Too many to count," said Ranger Blair. "These days, the lighthouse watches over fishing boats and pleasure boats. But when she was built, Lucy guided big trading ships in and out of the bay. They'd sail to India...China. Be gone for a year, sometimes more."

"That's a long time," said Amy.

"Especially when you're living on a cramped wooden ship," said the ranger. "There's a model of one in the museum. You'll see it on the tour."

Sarah loved the cozy keeper's cottage. It was full of things from Lucy's past. The model boat. Oil lamps and life preservers. Keepers' diaries.

Sarah read one entry:

January 19, 1865. As the tide rose today, the sea broke over the rocks. It washed away every moveable thing. It flooded our house! But we are safe in the light tower.

Good old Lucy, thought Sarah.

Ranger Blair pointed to an old rowboat and oars. "This is how keepers got to the mainland," she explained.

"Wow!" said Jo Ann. "They rowed the whole way?"

"When the weather allowed," said the ranger. "Mostly it didn't. A keeper's life was lonely. No neighbors. No mail service. No telephone."

"No TV?" Lauren pretended to be shocked.

Ranger Blair laughed. "No TV. Not in the old days. And not now either."

Sarah tried to imagine herself all alone on the island. "Are *you* lonely?" she blurted out. Then she blushed. She couldn't believe she had asked such a nosy question!

The ranger didn't seem to mind. "I'm only here summers. Park's closed in winter," she said. She motioned toward a crowd of sightseers. "I get lots of day visitors. And Ida Lewis keeps me company."

"Who's that, another ranger?" asked Marsha.

"No. My cat," said Ranger Blair. "Named after a famous Rhode Island lighthouse keeper. Saved a lot of people in her day."

Sarah felt shy about asking another question. But she wanted to know more about the cat. "Can we meet her? Your cat, I mean?"

"Up to her," said Ranger Blair. "Ida Lewis goes where she pleases. She may come find you. Or you may never see her at all!"

3

At snack time the Brownie Girl Scouts crowded around some old wooden picnic tables near the keeper's cottage.

"There's more trail mix," announced Jo Ann. "Want some, Sarah?"

"Uh...no thanks," Sarah said absently. A sudden movement on the cottage roof had caught her eye. Was that a cat's tail flicking back and forth—right there where the main roof hung over the porch roof? It was the perfect place for an afternoon catnap.

"What are you looking at?" asked Jo Ann.

"Ida Lewis, I think," Sarah replied.

Sure enough, a second later, a silvery-gray cat stood up and stretched. She leaped gracefully to a tree that stood near the porch. Then she backed down the trunk.

"Here, kitty, kitty, kitty," called Lauren.

"Here, Ida Lewis. Come here, kitty," called Marsha and both Krissys.

The cat ignored them. Tail high, she padded straight over to Sarah. She sniffed the fingers Sarah offered. Leaped into her lap. Turned around twice. And lay down.

Sarah was thrilled. Ida Lewis had chosen her! She scratched behind the cat's velvety ears and under her pointed chin.

The cat purred like a motorboat.

"Oooooh! Lucky you," said Corrie.

"Luck, nothing!" said Krissy S. "Animals always love Sarah!"

Sarah looked down. She felt shy being the center of attention. She was glad when Mrs. Q. called, "It will be low tide soon, girls. That's the best time to explore tide pools. We can look for the things we studied in our guidebook."

"And we can try out our water snoopers!" said Krissy A.

The Brownies had made their snoopers for the Water Everywhere Try-It. It was easy. Sarah had made hers from an empty coffee can. First she'd taken off the top and bottom lids. Then she'd put clear plastic wrap over one end and held it in place with a rubber band.

"I'm going to use my snooper to look for sea stars," said Lauren.

"I'm going to use mine to find shipwreck treasure!" said Amy.

But first, Krissy A.'s mom went over the safety rules. She was their lifeguard. Then the girls changed into old sneakers, got their water snoopers, and hurried down to the shore.

Ida Lewis followed, a silvery shadow at Sarah's heels.

"Hey, I thought *I* was your buddy," Jo Ann teased.

"You are," said Sarah. "Ida Lewis is our private guide. She's going to show us the best tide pool. Aren't you, girl?"

Sarah had meant it as a joke. But suddenly Ida Lewis stalked ahead.

Jo Ann giggled. "Lead on, trusty guide!"

The cat picked her way over the rocks. She stopped by a large pool.

"I guess this is it," said Sarah. She lay on her stomach and put the plastic-covered end of her snooper in the water. Then she peered through the other end.

Jo Ann did the same. "Wow! This snooper really works!" she exclaimed. "I can see everything in here!"

"Me too," said Sarah. "It's a tiny sea world. Like an aquarium—only better!"

Curtains of dark greenish seaweed draped the walls of the pool. Tiny fish darted back and forth. There were little snails feeding off the seaweed, and miniature volcano-shaped things fastened to the rocks. Periwinkles and limpets! Sarah remembered them from the guidebook.

She scanned the bottom of the pool. "A sea star! Look, Jo Ann!" Sarah was so excited she dropped her snooper.

A little later, Jo Ann saw something
special, too. A spiny sea urchin,
hanging under a rock ledge.

The girls explored the shore for nearly an
hour. At some point, Ida Lewis left them.
The cat clearly knew her way around the
island. Sarah just hoped she'd see her again,
before the troop left in the morning.

"The tide's coming in," called Krissy A.'s
mom. "We'd better start back."

Sarah took a quick peek under one last
rock. And there was her best find of the day.
A tiny green crab! It waved its claws at her,
as if it were ready to fight.

Sarah laughed. "You're pretty brave for
such a little guy." She picked the crab up
carefully. "Jo Ann! Come see what I
found!" she called.

Jo Ann came up behind her. "What is it?"
Sarah spun around and held out the crab.

"Yikes!" Jo Ann jumped back so fast she
lost her balance and sat down—in the
middle of a puddle.

"Sorry, Jo Ann! I didn't mean to scare
you," said Sarah. She put down the crab,
which scuttled away.

"I wasn't scared!" Jo Ann said quickly. "I was just a little—um—surprised. That's all." She got to her feet. "Yuck! I am one soggy doggy. Good thing it's time to go back."

The Brownies headed for the lighthouse. Corrie, Marsha, and Krissy S. had collected pretty bits of smooth sea glass to take home. They were all different colors. Amy had found a worn piece of china.

"This came from a shipwreck! I'm sure of it," she said. "One minute it was a plate on the captain's table. Then crash, splash! It's in the ocean—lost for a hundred years."

Sarah laughed along with the other girls. Then suddenly they heard the toot of the ferry's horn.

"Last ferry!" called Amy. "Now the island is ours. We're all alone!"

Sarah wished Amy hadn't reminded her. She'd been having so much fun. But now they really were all alone, and far from home. And soon it would be dark. It was going to be a long night.

4

The Brownie Girl Scouts ate dinner
outside in the picnic area. And no one felt
shy about asking for seconds—not even
Sarah.

"This sea air sure gave you guys an
appetite," said Mrs. Q. "I brought tons of
hot dogs—and every last one is gone!"

"Gee, I only had two," said Marsha. "Or
was it three? No. I think two."

"Forget hot dogs," said Amy. "Here's the

important question. What's for dessert?"

"S'mores, of course," said Mrs. Q. "But it looks as if we might get rained out."

While they were eating, dark clouds had rolled in. Now a sudden gust of wind sent their paper napkins flying.

Ranger Blair joined them. "Storm's coming. Going to be a big one," she said.

"Thanks for the warning," said Mrs. Q.

The Brownies put out the cook fire and chased down the flying trash. They made a quick stop at the rest room, then headed for the lighthouse.

The wind was blowing harder now. And the sky was the color of an old bruise. Sarah was glad to go inside. She patted the wall on her way in. What was another thunderstorm to Lucy. She'd stood up to hurricanes!

The round room was cozy. The Brownies got out cards and jacks. Amy braided Lauren's hair. Corrie made patterns with her sea glass. And Sarah and Marsha played cat's cradle with a piece of string.

"Would anyone like to climb to the top of the tower?" asked Mrs. Q. "The moms and I can take you up—four at a time."

Everyone wanted to go. So four by four they climbed the stairs again. Sarah and Jo Ann went with Amy, Corrie, and Marsha's mom.

Wow, thought Sarah. Everything sure looks different from this afternoon!

The sky was full of dark clouds, and the ocean was gray and choppy. The gulls were gone. And so were the boats.

"Wild!" said Jo Ann. "I love storms—as long as I'm safe inside!"

"I don't mind them," said Sarah. "But my cat Nora does. She hides under the bed."

"I guess she's a scaredy-cat," joked Jo Ann. "Not brave like us. Right?"

"Right." Sarah smiled weakly. Sure, I'm brave, she thought. Until the lights go out.

Suddenly Lucy's beacon came on. It sent a powerful beam of white light over the sea. Like a giant flashlight, thought Sarah.

"All right! Lucy's on the job," said Amy.

"It's barely sunset. I thought the light came on at night," said Corrie.

"Look at the sky," said Jo Ann. "It's so dark, it might as well be night."

"Hey, that reminds me of a game," said Amy. "It's called 'It Was a Dark and Stormy Night.' Want to play?"

"Sure!" said Corrie and Jo Ann.

They started down the stairs. Sarah trailed behind with Marsha's mom, a little worried. What if to play you had to turn out all the lights?

Luckily, it wasn't that kind of game. Amy had everyone sit in a circle. Then she began a story. "It was a dark and stormy night," she said. "A family was driving down a lonely country road, when suddenly—" She tapped Krissy A., who was sitting beside her. "Now you go on."

"Um. Suddenly, a huge tree fell in front of the car," said Krissy. "It blocked the road. But luckily—" She tapped Lauren.

"Luckily, the family had a pet beaver!" said Lauren. "It chewed through that tree like a buzz saw. But then—"

The story went on around the circle. Each girl added to it. And the plot got sillier and sillier until everyone had the giggles.

Then it was time for bed. The Brownies changed into pajamas and rolled out their sleeping bags. Sarah carefully tucked her flashlight under her pillow.

"Could I read a story before we go to sleep?" asked Krissy S. "It's from this brochure I found in the museum. And it's about the Point Lucy Lighthouse."

"I hope it's a ghost story!" said Amy.

"It is," said Krissy. "And it takes place on another dark and stormy night."

Sarah hugged her knees. Krissy S. was such an actress. She was great at reading out loud.

" 'In November of 1846,' " Krissy began in a low voice, " 'Joshua Hayes was hired as a cabin boy on the trading ship, the *Abigail*. But two days before he was to set sail, he dreamed of a storm and a shipwreck, and of drowning sailors crying out in the dark.

" 'Joshua told the *Abigail*'s captain about his dream. He begged him not to set sail. The captain just laughed. The *Abigail* left on time. But Joshua Hayes was not on board. He hid in the woods until the ship was far from the bay.

" 'That night there was a terrible storm. The next day, pieces of the ship washed up around the Point Lucy Lighthouse. Joshua's dream had come true.

"'There were no survivors. But some people believe that the *Abigail*'s sailors still haunt the island, and that whenever there's a storm, you can hear them calling out in the night.'"

Krissy S. paused. "'Listen carefully,'" she whispered. "'And you may hear them, too.'"

For a moment no one spoke. Then Amy broke the silence. "Oooooh! Great story!"

Some of the other girls nodded. But Sarah just sat there. A story like that was not what she needed right before lights-out!

To her relief, Mrs. Q. turned off the main lights but switched on her flashlight. The room would not be dark after all!

Mrs. Q. and Krissy A.'s mom talked softly. Sarah closed her eyes. The sound of their voices mixed with the sound of the wind and the waves. Before she knew it, Sarah was asleep.

5

Sarah woke up terrified. For a moment she wasn't sure where she was. Then she remembered—Lucy. But she couldn't see anything! Mrs. Q. must have turned off her flashlight before going to sleep. The room was totally dark.

Outside, thunder boomed and echoed. The wind howled. And the surf roared against the rocky shore.

It's okay, Sarah told herself. The storm woke me up, that's all. I'm with my friends.

And nothing in the dark will hurt me.

There was a big clap of thunder.

Then she heard it. Something moving. Something close by!

There was another thunderclap. Then heavy breathing—like a monster in a scary movie.

Sarah reached under her pillow and grabbed her flashlight. She pointed it at the sound, flicked it on, and saw...Mrs. Q.?

Mrs. Q. looked as surprised as Sarah. She seemed about to say something, when thunder boomed right overhead.

Mrs. Q. winced. She took a deep breath, then she grinned. "I'm sorry if I woke you, Sarah," she whispered.

Sarah lowered her flashlight. "That's okay. I really think it was the storm."

"I can never sleep on nights like this," Mrs. Q. told her. "Ever since I was a kid, I've hated loud noises. And thunder always startles me, even though I know it's nothing to be afraid of."

Mrs. Q. sat up. "When I was little, I hid in the closet during thunderstorms. At least now my fear doesn't stop me from doing anything I want to do."

Sarah was amazed. Mrs. Q. was scared of something! And she didn't mind admitting it. She could even laugh about it.

Maybe, thought Sarah, just maybe Mrs. Q. will understand how I feel about the dark. "Thunder doesn't bother me," she said softly. "But...well...I *am* afraid of the dark."

"You're not alone," said Mrs. Q. "I don't know anyone who's not scared of something."

"Spiders," said a voice.

"What?" said Sarah and Mrs. Q. together.

Jo Ann sat up. "Spiders—that's what I'm scared of. That's why I freaked out when you showed me the crab, Sarah. For a second I thought it was a giant spider!"

"Why didn't you say so?" asked Sarah.

"I thought you'd laugh," said Jo Ann. "*You're* not scared of spiders, are you?"

"No," said Sarah. "Just the dark." She stopped in surprise. That was the second time she'd said it. And she wasn't nearly as embarrassed as before.

There was another huge crash of thunder, and the other girls woke up.

"Hey, what's this? A party?" said Amy.

"Not really," said Mrs. Q. "We're just talking about things that scare us."

"Getting shots at the doctor's. That's what scares me," said Krissy S.

"I'm afraid of big dogs," said Marsha. "Big dogs with big, sharp teeth!"

"I'm scared of vampires," said Amy.

"What?" said Jo Ann. "I thought you liked ghosts and stuff like that."

"Ghosts, yes. Vampires, no. There's a difference," Amy said seriously.

"At least vampires aren't real," said Lauren. "But bats! Ugh!"

"What about moths?" Corrie said. "I don't like the powdery stuff on their wings."

"Me either," said Amy. "It comes off on your hands if you try to catch them."

"Gross," said Marsha. "But here's something grosser. Already chewed gum!"

"The skin on chocolate pudding!" said Krissy A.

"The smell of my old sneakers!" said Amy.

That cracked everyone up, and Sarah felt better. She was still afraid of the dark. But at least she wasn't the only scaredy-cat in the troop.

"As long as we're all awake, how about a midnight snack?" said Mrs. Q. "We can't make S'mores. But we can eat the ingredients!"

Everybody cheered.

Mrs. Q. turned on the lights. She got out graham crackers, chocolate bars, and marshmallows.

"Yum!" said Amy. "Hey, Corrie. Want to trade your chocolate for my graham cracker? I'll even throw in a marshmallow."

"Not a chance," said Corrie.

"This is fun," Jo Ann said to Sarah. "It's like a giant slumber party—only better!"

Sarah grinned. "A slumber party in a lighthouse on an island in a thunderstorm. That's pretty special, all right."

6

When the last square of chocolate was gone, most of the girls crawled back into their sleeping bags. But not Sarah.

"Um...Mrs. Q.?" she said softly. "I've got to go to the bathroom. Sorry."

"That's okay, Sarah. I'll take you," said Mrs. Q. She looked around the group. "Anyone else have to use the rest room?"

Jo Ann and Krissy S. raised their hands.

The four of them slipped on sweatshirts and sneakers. Then Sarah and Mrs. Q.

grabbed their flashlights, and they all went downstairs.

Sarah stopped in the doorway. A shiver of fear ran down her spine.

The storm was over. But the moon and stars were still covered by clouds. And the lighthouse beacon only shone out to sea. The island was very, very dark.

"Come on, Sarah," Jo Ann called.

Sarah switched on her flashlight. Her heart was pounding as she followed the others to the rest room. She was careful not to look to the left or right of the path. She was too afraid of what might be hiding just outside her flashlight beam.

On the way back to the lighthouse, the path seemed even darker. Then suddenly there was a terrible howl.

"Wh-what was that?" Jo Ann's voice shook.

The howl came again. High and trembly. And too creepy to be human.

Krissy S. clutched Sarah's arm. "It's a ghost. The drowned sailors are after us!"

"That's no ghost," said Sarah. "That's a cat! It's Ida Lewis, and she's in trouble!" She turned to Mrs. Q. "We have to help her."

"Of course," said Mrs. Q. "Come on, we'll follow the sound."

Ida Lewis yowled again.

"The keeper's cottage!" said Sarah.

They hurried as fast as they could.

"I bet she's on the porch roof—where she was this morning," said Sarah.

She pointed her flashlight at the spot. So did Mrs. Q.

There was Ida Lewis. Cold, wet—and very unhappy. She yowled again.

"She must have gone up there to get out of the storm," said Mrs. Q. "But why doesn't she come down the same way she did before?"

She shined her light at the tree. A big branch lay on the ground, snapped off by the wind.

"There's the answer," said Jo Ann. "That was the branch Ida Lewis used to get on and off the roof."

"We'll need a ladder to get her," said Mrs. Q. "I'm sure Ranger Blair has one."

"Wait," said Sarah. "Maybe I can talk Ida Lewis down. Get her to jump into my arms."

"Okay. Let's give it a try," said Mrs. Q.

They shined their flashlights at the cat.

"Here, Ida Lewis. Come, kitty, kitty," Sarah called in a gentle voice. "Don't worry. I'll catch you."

Ida Lewis turned away. She yowled again.

"Something's wrong. She sounds more upset than ever," said Jo Ann.

"You're right," said Sarah. "Maybe we're blinding her with our flashlights." She took a deep breath. "Let's try turning them off."

They switched off their flashlights.

The darkness was so complete Sarah could almost feel it surrounding her like a heavy coat. For a moment she froze. Then she thought of Ida Lewis. This was no time to panic.

Mrs. Q. sensed how scared she was. "We're right here beside you, Sarah," she said softly.

Sarah took a slow, steady breath. To her

surprise, she began to see outlines. Her eyes were adjusting to the dark.

She talked to the cat, telling her everything was going to be okay. And she called Ida's name over and over.

Ida Lewis stopped yowling. Then finally she jumped. Right into Sarah's waiting arms.

"Hurray!" Krissy S. and Jo Ann cheered.

"You did it, Sarah!" said Mrs. Q.

Sarah cradled Ida Lewis in her arms. "It's okay, kitty. You're safe now."

Mrs. Q. patted Sarah's shoulder. "Ranger Blair's lights are out, and we're so close to the lighthouse. Let's take the cat with us."

Sarah beamed.

Back inside, she wrapped Ida Lewis snugly in her sweatshirt. Then she cuddled the cat until she was warm and dry—and purring loudly. In a few minutes they were both fast asleep.

7

The morning was already half gone when Sarah woke up. And she was not the only sleepyhead. After all the excitement of the storm and the midnight party, everyone had slept late.

Sarah yawned and stretched.

So did Ida Lewis. Then she touched noses with Sarah.

"You want to go out, don't you kitty?" said Sarah.

The cat padded over to
the door and waited.

Sarah opened it, followed
Ida downstairs, and opened
the outside door.

The cat slipped out, a silver streak against
the green grass. Then Sarah went back
upstairs.

Over breakfast, Jo Ann and Krissy S. told
the story of Ida Lewis's rescue. Krissy made
it sound so dramatic, Sarah hardly knew
where to look or what to say.

"You're a hero, Sarah!" said Lauren.

Sarah was embarrassed. "I guess I did
help Ida Lewis," she admitted. "But I was
scared to death out there in the dark."

"Maybe so," said Mrs. Q. "But you
didn't let it stop you! That's what courage
is all about."

Sarah grinned. "I guess I was brave and didn't even know it!"

After the Brownies cleaned up and packed their bags, they raced outside. There was time for one last visit to the shore before the ferry came.

Sarah went back to the tide pool that Ida Lewis had shown her. It looked almost the same as before. But the storm had wedged something new under one of the rocks. A small piece of driftwood.

Sarah picked it up. The wood had been worn smooth and silvery gray by the waves.

She turned it over in her palm. Then she looked a little closer. It was shaped exactly like a curled-up cat.

❊   ❊   ❊

Sarah stood at the back rail of the Point Lucy ferry. The boat was heading away from the island. But for now she could still see the lighthouse.

Sarah reached into her pocket. She stroked the satiny back of her little driftwood cat.

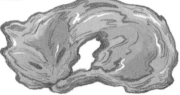

"Good-bye, Ida Lewis. Good-bye, Ranger Blair," she said. "And good-bye, Lucy. I'll never forget you."

Then the ferry turned into the bay, and the tall, white tower disappeared from sight.

Girl Scout Ways

Sarah and her friends used water snoopers to explore the tide pools around the Point Lucy Lighthouse. You can make your own water snooper, too, to use the next time you visit a tide pool, pond, or river.

- Here's what you'll need: a large can (like a coffee can), clear plastic wrap, and a big rubber band.

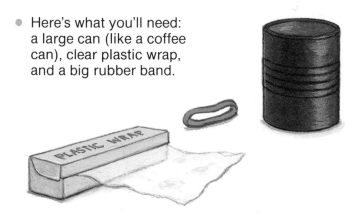

- First have someone help you remove both ends of the can.

- Next, tear off a piece of plastic wrap and place it over one end of the can. Use the rubber band to hold the plastic in place.

To use your water snooper, just dip the end with the plastic wrap into the water and look through the open end. You'll be amazed at all the things you'll see!